Y4

Painting Party

D1342158

Follow the Glitter Girls' latest adventures!
Collect the other fantastic books in the series:

Caroline Plaisted

Painting Party

SCHOLASTIC

Scholastic Children's Books,
Commonwealth House, 1-19 New Oxford Street,
London WC1A 1NU, UK
a division of Scholastic Ltd

London ~ New York ~ Toronto ~ Sydney ~ Auckland
Mexico City ~ New Delhi ~ Hong Kong

Published in the UK by Scholastic Ltd, 2003

Copyright © Caroline Plaisted, 2003

ISBN 0 439 98175 1

Typeset by Falcon Oast Graphic Art Ltd
Printed and bound in Great Britain by Cox & Wyman Ltd, Reading, Berkshire

2 4 6 8 10 9 7 5 3 1

Chapter 1

It was Monday night and the Glitter Girls were off to the Energy Zone with Meg's brother Jack and his best friend Nick.

"Wonder what we'll do tonight?" Charly asked, as they hurried along, eager to be there.

"Hope you're not going to do lots of girly singing and dancing," moaned Nick.

"Yuck!" agreed Jack.

"Well, even if we are, you two don't have to do it with us, do you?" exclaimed Zoe.

"No!" the other Glitter Girls agreed.

"No thanks," cried Jack. "It's bad enough having to listen to you lot in Meg's bedroom."

Nick laughed. "Yes – we've heard you!"

"Oh, sure," said Meg. "I bet you have!"

"We have," insisted Jack. "We know how much you like Britney Spears." He gave Nick a knowing look and they both started sniggering.

The Glitter Girls looked sideways at each other. Did this mean that Nick and Jack listened in on the Glitter Girls' secret meetings?

"Anyway," said Flo, trying to look as if she didn't care. "We're here now. Just make sure you don't sit anywhere near us!"

"Fat chance," Jack replied and ran into the hall with Nick.

"Boys – they're so annoying!" Hannah giggled.

"Yeah," her friends all agreed, laughing.

"They're *really* annoying," Meg said. "And it looks like we'd better be more careful about our meetings in future."

★　♥　★　♥　★　♥　★

"Evening all!" Danny called the Energy Zone to order and everyone grabbed a chair and formed their usual circle.

"Right – we've got lots to do tonight," Danny explained. "First, can I remind you all to sign yourselves in. . ."

There was a mumble of agreement from everyone in the hall.

". . .and then before you all get on with your own stuff this evening, can I remind you we've got to organize ourselves for Easter."

"Easter?" Charly asked. "What's happening then?"

"Well, I thought we could do a bit of celebrating this Easter – seeing as the Energy Zone will be five years old!" Danny explained.

"Yeah!" everyone cheered.

"So –" Danny gestured for everyone to quieten down – "I thought we could have a Fun Day on Easter Saturday."

"What's that?" Jack wanted to know.

"It's a day when everyone has fun, *der-brain!*" Meg retorted.

Everyone laughed and Jack blushed, furious

at his little sister for showing him up in public.

"Exactly," Danny said, smiling. "But *how* we have fun is up to you to decide. "

"So who's coming to this Fun Day?" Charly asked. "Just us lot?"

"Us lot and I hope lots of other kids who might want to find out more about the Energy Zone and perhaps come and join in with us after the Easter holidays," Danny replied.

"Cool!" Flo grinned. "Can we have a disco?"

"Yes – we could do the music!" Jack and Nick said together.

"Even if he is my brother," Meg said to the rest of the Energy Zone, "they'd actually be quite good at it."

"Disco it is then," Danny said, writing it down on his clipboard.

"We'll need food and the hall will need decorating for the disco, won't it?" Meg said.

"We could do the decorating!" Flo volunteered, pointing to her four best friends. "I'm sure we could turn this hall into somewhere really cool." She looked round at the dreary dark walls and hoped that she was right.

"Go Glitter!" the four other Glitter Girls agreed and Danny wrote that down too.

"OK," Danny said. "So what other ideas have you got?"

"We could have a treasure hunt!" suggested Amy, one of the older girls.

"I know!" Fizz, a friend of Jack's and Nick's, shot his hand up. "My mum works at Choc City – she might be able to get us some Easter eggs for the treasure hunt!"

"Nice one!" shouted Senami.

"Yes – bags I help lay the treasure hunt out!" giggled Jack.

"Yeah, *right* – I don't think so," said Meg, picturing her brother munching his way through the chocolate as he did.

"Precisely," Danny laughed. "If you can get some Easter eggs, Fizz, that would be great –

but I think I'll be in charge of putting the treasure hunt out."

"I could run a pool tournament," Will offered.

Everyone nodded in agreement because they knew that Will was really good at pool and had already played in a local tournament against adults.

"What about all the food and stuff that we'll need?" Chenzira, Senami's best friend, wondered.

"We could put up a list – you know crisps, rolls, Coke," Meg suggested. "Then we could put our names next to the things we are going to bring."

"Good idea," agreed Danny.

"Danny?" Ria, who had only just joined the Energy Zone herself, put her hand up. "How are we going to let people know about Fun Day?"

"I thought you lot could tell your friends at school about it – spread the word?" Danny replied.

"We need posters!" Flo declared. "Then we could put them up around town and get loads more children interested."

"Good idea," Danny confirmed. "But I'm afraid we don't have any spare cash for printing posters. In fact, I was hoping that we might be able to raise some money at Fun Day to help us out next term."

"Why don't we all make our own?" Ria suggested.

"Yes," said Meg. "As long as we make sure that each one has the same information on it."

"Sounds good to me," Danny agreed, picking up his clipboard and pen. "So what does the poster need to say?"

"What the event is!" Hannah suggested.

"And where it is!" Zoe agreed.

"How much it costs to come!" Charly added.

"Who it's run by!" Flo offered.

"And when it is!" Meg concluded.

"Nice one, girls," Danny grinned. "I think I

can answer those for you. The date is Easter Saturday – the 19th. The place is the community hall, as you know. There'll be a £1 entry fee that'll include entry to the treasure hunt, and it's all in aid of the Energy Zone and getting people interested in the fun stuff we all get up to!"

"We can start making the posters straight away," Meg said, flipping her own handy note-book from her pocket and scribbling down the information.

"OK," Danny looked at his watch. "I think that's enough about Fun Day for tonight. Let's get the Energy Zone started properly! Munchies and a drink in about an hour."

"Yes!" everyone at the Energy Zone yelled as they headed off in different directions, still talk-ing about what they were going to do for Fun Day.

Chapter 2

Straight away, the Glitter Girls got together with the other girls to talk about Fun Day.

"I hope I find some of the eggs in the treasure hunt!" Flo said, already anticipating how good the chocolate would taste.

"So do I," agreed Charly.

"I wish we could have an Easter bonnet competition!" said Hannah. "They had one at ballet last year and it was really good."

"The boys would hate it, though!" Amy said, laughing.

"Good point," agreed Zoe. "But it would be nice to have some kind of competition, wouldn't it. . ."

"Hmm," said Meg thoughtfully. "Yes. . ."

"Yes what?" asked Charly, seeing the twinkle in her friend's eye.

"What if we had a competition to do with Easter eggs," Meg suggested.

"What kind of competition?" her friends asked.

"How about we ask Danny if we could all decorate an Easter egg?" Meg said.

"Decorate?" Ria asked. "You mean like icing a cake?"

"No," Zoe said. "You get an egg and then blow the yolk out of it – it's really yucky!"

"Yes, and once you've got an empty shell," Hannah explained, "you paint or decorate the shell."

"Hey, that sounds great!" Senami said, and the other girls agreed.

"Let's ask Danny later if it's OK," Meg suggested.

"So – anyone else got any other ideas?" Zoe asked.

Along with the other girls, the Glitter Girls

spent a happy hour chatting through lots of other ideas for Fun Day. When they stopped for their snack and a drink later on, they told Danny about the Easter egg competition and he thought it was a good idea.

"Any ideas about who can judge it?" he asked.

The Glitter Girls hadn't thought about that.

"Tell you what – why don't you all give it a think and come back to me next week?"

There was a murmur of agreement from the Energy Zone.

"OK," Danny looked at his watch. "We've got twenty minutes left before home time – who fancies a quick game of indoor hockey?"

"Yes!" was the general response.

"Boys against girls!" Jack yelled, grinning at his friends.

"No contest!" Zoe called back.

And the game began.

★ ♥ ★ ♥ ★ ♥ ★

RAT-tat-tat!

"Who's there?" Zoe whispered through her bedroom door.

"GG!"

Immediately, she opened the door to find her four friends eager to come inside. It had been pouring with rain as they'd walked over to Zoe's house so they were all desperate to warm up and dry off in Zoe's lovely cosy room.

"Phew!" said Meg. "No danger of my idiot brother lurking about here!"

"No," Zoe smiled – she had two older sisters who were happy to leave the Glitter Girls in peace.

"Still – I shouldn't think Jack and Nick are feeling that proud of themselves after we trashed them at hockey last night!" sniggered Zoe.

Once Meg, Flo, Charly and Hannah had settled down on the assortment of beanbags and rugs in Zoe's room, Zoe grabbed a big biscuit tin from her desk and then handed it round to her friends.

"Here – have one of these," she offered.

"What's this?" Charly asked, peering inside the tin. "Hey, yum!"

"Scrummy!" agreed Hannah, grabbing a delicious-looking cookie covered in tiny Smarties and munching on it.

"Who made these?" Meg asked.

"Me and my sisters," Zoe said. "I was thinking about the egg competition and it got me in the mood for decorating something."

"I haven't a clue what to do about my decorated egg," Charly sighed.

"I haven't even thought about it yet," Hannah said.

"Well, I think we should do an egg as a team," Meg exclaimed. "Then we won't have to compete with each other, will we?"

"Good idea!" agreed Flo.

"Eggs-actly!" giggled Hannah.

"Eggs-citing!" sniggered Charly, pushing her pink glasses back up on her nose.

"Eggs-tremely!" Meg agreed.

The Glitter Girls collapsed with laughter at their jokes.

"Seriously, though – what could we do?" Zoe asked.

"Something that looks like the Glitter Girls did it!" Flo suggested.

"That's easy then!" decided Hannah. "Let's do us!"

"Us?" Meg wondered.

"Oh, I get it!" Charly said. "We could each decorate an egg to look like us – the Glitter Girls!"

"Brilliant!" said Flo. "We could do our jackets and everything!"

"Cool!" agreed Zoe.

"That's sorted then!" Meg said. "So now all we've got to do is get wool and stuff to do our hair and then we can get *cracking* – get it?"

The four other girls groaned at Meg's terrible pun.

"Tell you what," said Hannah, "I'll ask my mum if she can help us and maybe find us some wool and some denim."

"It's going to be hard work making the hall look like a disco," Zoe sighed.

"We'll certainly need to give it a bit of a makeover – it's so boring," Hannah said.

"We can make streamers," Flo suggested.

"Good idea." Meg wrote it down.

"And get some of those glittery balloons from the party shop in town," said Charly.

"If we got some pretty fairy lights as well, I'm sure we could make the hall look much more like a disco," Zoe offered.

"Course we can," Flo said confidently.

"Another good idea," agreed Meg, writing notes in her little pink notebook.

"So what are we going to do about these posters?" Charly asked.

"I thought we could start on them now," Flo suggested, pulling a wad of paper and a load of felt pens and gel pens from her purple rucksack.

"What was it we had to put on each one?" Hannah wondered.

"Here, I wrote it down: date, time, place, entry fee, who it's for and who's organizing it!" Meg read from her notebook.

"Let's get going then," Flo handed out the paper and spread the pens on the floor between them.

"Just one thing," Meg warned.

"What's that?" asked Charly.

"Don't forget to mention the egg decorating competition!" Meg reminded them.

"Course!" said Hannah. "The more who enter, the better!"

"Come on – let's get designing posters!" said Flo excitedly.

Flo loved art and she was soon creating

fantastic glittery letters on her poster. It gave the other Glitter Girls great ideas and an hour later, after drawing along to one of their favourite CDs, they sat back and admired their handiwork. Spread out in front of them were sparkly posters, decorated with wild fluorescent flowers and fabulous lettering.

"Danny should like these," Hannah said.

"I'm sure he will," Meg said. "We'd better leave them here – if we take them home in this weather they'll get ruined."

The rain was still pouring down outside Zoe's bedroom window.

"I'd better be going – I've still got some homework to do," said Hannah, gathering up her denim jacket and bag.

"Me too!" the others agreed.

"It's horrible out there!" sighed Charly.

"It's hardly stopped all day," agreed Meg.

"Aren't we going to get soaked?" Hannah asked.

"We'll just have to run for it!" Flo suggested.

Chapter 3

It rained all the next day as well. At school, the Glitter Girls had to stay inside at break time and lunch because it was just too wet to go out. But the Glitter Girls kept themselves busy by making plans for their decorations for the Fun Day disco and talking about how they were going to create their eggs.

"The only thing about the fairy lights idea is that we'd need lots of sets of lights to have any impact in the hall, wouldn't we?" Meg pondered.

"Well – we've all got at least one set each at home, haven't we? You know, the ones for decorating the Christmas tree," Charly pointed out. "We could all bring those."

"We've got two sets," Zoe confirmed.

"So have we," agreed Flo.

"And us," said Hannah.

"OK," said Meg, noting things down in her notebook. "But we'd better make sure Danny thinks it's OK. We can ask him tonight."

★ ♥ ★ ♥ ★ ♥ ★

The Glitter Girls hurried to the Energy Zone that night, huddled under their umbrellas. Jack and Nick ran ahead of them, shrouded by the hoods of their waterproof jackets. It was raining so hard, it seemed almost dark. When the seven of them arrived at the hall, they ran towards the door, only to crash straight into Danny.

"Whoa!" he cried. "Steady, you lot!"

"Come on," said Jack. "Open up, Danny!"

"Yes – it's cold out here," Nick said. "And we're getting soaked."

"Ah," said Danny. "Well there's a bit of a problem with that I'm afraid."

"What's that?" Meg asked, realizing that other

members of the Energy Zone were huddled behind Danny and even more of them were hurrying up the road towards the town centre.

"There's a bit of a problem with the hall," Danny explained. "We've got to go to the church hall down the road instead."

"The church hall?" Charly wondered aloud. "Why?"

Danny pulled his clipboard out from under his coat. "I'm just going to put this notice on the door telling everyone where we are. Then we can go to the other hall and I'll explain everything there."

Ten minutes later, the Energy Zone dripped their way into the church hall – not looking as if they had any energy left at all!

"Come on – sign in and then grab a chair," Danny suggested.

"So, what's going on?" one of the older boys asked, sitting down.

"All this lovely weather we've been having over the past couple of days has caused a problem, I'm afraid," Danny explained.

"What kind of problem?" Flo wanted to know.

"It's the flat roof on the hall," Danny said. "It's always been a bit dodgy and the council have been intending to replace it for years. Anyway, all this rain has finally finished it off. I got a phone call this morning telling me that the rain had poured through the roof and brought the ceiling down."

"Wow!" Jack said. "Can we go and see it? It must be a real mess!"

"That's typical of you!" Meg sighed, folding her arms in disgust at her brother's excitement.

"Well, it certainly is a mess," Danny replied. "And because it rained non-stop, not only did the ceiling come down, but the rain penetrated the walls, so they're damaged too."

"Disaster!" exclaimed Charly.

"Total disaster, actually," Danny said, "because it means that major repairs are going to have to be done."

"So does that mean we won't be able to use the hall for our meetings for a couple of weeks?" Zoe asked.

"Certainly does," Danny confirmed. "Only not just for a couple of weeks – it could be months."

"Months?" Hannah cried. "But Fun Day is in five weeks! We need the hall for the disco!"

"And the pool tournament!" Nick exclaimed.

"If the hall isn't going to be ready for Fun Day, though," Jack began, "can't we just have it here instead? I mean, it's OK, isn't it? We're here tonight, aren't we?"

"But we need the Rec too – for the treasure hunt!" Nick reminded him.

"Exactly!" Charly said.

"It would certainly be better to hold it in our usual hall," Danny agreed. "I mean, we could have the Fun Day here – if it's available – but, like Nick says, we won't be able to have the treasure hunt. The work on the hall is going to be quite major – what with the roof and ceiling as well as the walls. And even if the walls don't need replastering, they need to dry out."

"Oh no!" the Glitter Girls sighed, and there were mumblings of agreement from other members of the Energy Zone as everyone sat there feeling really disappointed.

"Is there no way it can be fixed in five weeks?" Meg suggested.

"Unlikely," Danny said, "but we can always hope. I've got a meeting with the council later this week and I'll be able to tell you what they say at our next meeting on Friday."

The room was quiet – not at all like the usually boisterous Energy Zone.

"Come on, you guys – let's not get too down-hearted," Danny said encouragingly. "Who's got any more ideas for Fun Day?"

"Has anyone had any ideas about who could judge the egg decorating?" Meg said, looking around the room half-heartedly.

No one put their hand up. Everyone still looked pretty fed up.

"Actually, I had an idea about that myself," Danny put in. "A mate of mine – Joe – is an art teacher at a secondary school on the other side of town. I was going to ask him to give us a hand with the Fun Day anyway, so I thought he might be able to judge the competition. What do you guys reckon?"

There were mumbles of agreement from the group. Flo nodded enthusiastically and everyone agreed it would be a good idea to have an art teacher as a judge.

Then Jonny, one of the older boys, put his hand up. "Danny? My dad wondered if you wanted to borrow his big barbecue?" Jonny asked.

"Hmm, yeah – could be good," Danny said, nodding.

"But we can't have a barbecue on the pavement, can we?" Charly sighed.

"No," said Danny thoughtfully, "but maybe we could just about squeeze one on to the patch of grass outside – or perhaps borrow someone's garden down the road."

"But that just wouldn't be the same," said Meg.

There was a groan of disappointment from everyone as they realized that was true.

The Glitter Girls shook their heads sadly. It looked as if Fun Day wasn't going to be so much fun after all.

Chapter 4

It was a really boring week for the Glitter Girls. They didn't seem to have anything special to look forward to now, or even to keep them busy without something fun to organize, although they did spend one afternoon blowing the yolks out of the eggs they were going to decorate. But once the eggs were empty, the girls didn't have the heart to finish them – just in case there wasn't a competition after all.

On Thursday afternoon, though, Charly's mum, Mrs Fisher, came to meet them from school, as she often did.

"Thought you might like to see this," she said, handing the Glitter Girls a copy of the local paper as they climbed into the back of her car.

"What's in it?" Charly asked as she looked carefully at the front page.

"It's a couple of pages in," Mrs Fisher replied. "In the top right-hand corner."

"Hey, look!" Zoe said excitedly, leaning over Charly's shoulder to get a look at the article. "It's about the community hall: *'Heavy Rain Spells Disaster for Community'* "

"What does it say?" Meg wanted to know.

Zoe quickly scanned through the article and told them.

"It says that the council hopes to make the repairs over the next four weeks but that they won't be able to reopen the hall for at least six weeks!"

"Oh no – why's that?" Hannah asked.

Zoe looked down at the paper again to find out more.

"Oh. . ." she sighed. "They say they won't be able to decorate it until after Easter!"

"No way!" Hannah exclaimed. "Then it

definitely won't be ready for Fun Day."

"There must be something we can do about that!" Meg stated, a determined look in her eye.

"Like what?" Flo wanted to know. "Decorate it ourselves?"

"Yes! That's it!" Charly yelled.

"But how can we do that?" Zoe asked her friend.

"I remember seeing a programme once," Charly explained. "You must remember it! You know – when a group of people all got together to fix up a lighthouse."

"*Hit Squad!*" Meg remembered. "That's what it's called! It's when everyone gets together and helps with the painting and the curtains and stuff."

"Could we really do that?" Hannah asked.

"Yeah – if everyone at the Energy Zone took part," Flo said. "Then we could have a painting party!"

"Hey, girls!" Mrs Fisher called to them as she

pulled up outside her house. "Sorry to break up your discussion but we're home."

"We need a meeting!" Meg declared as the five friends got out of the car. "My house? After homework?"

"Go Glitter!" the other four confirmed.

★ ♥ ★ ♥ ★ ♥ ★

Two hours later, the Glitter Girls were deep in conversation in Meg's bedroom. They'd already checked to make sure that Jack was out of the house at football.

Meg was lying on her purple fleece floor-cushion, her notebook out in front of her.

"OK," she said. "So if the repair work is finished in four weeks, we've got a week to decorate the hall before Easter Saturday."

"But even if we all help," said Flo, "we'll only have the evenings, won't we? I mean we're at school all week – are we really going to have enough time?"

"We'll have all day too – we'll all be on holiday for Easter by then, remember!"

"Course!" Hannah smiled. "Perfect!"

"Do you think Danny will go for it?" Zoe asked.

"I'm sure we can persuade him. I mean, he's a teacher so he'll be on holiday too!" said Charly.

"Good job he gets the same holidays as us!" Flo grinned. "We can ask him when we next see him."

"So what do we need to get?" Meg said, making one of her famous lists. "If we plan it all out as much as we can now and show Danny how determined we are, how can he say no?"

The Glitter Girls grinned with approval.

"Paint!" Flo suggested. "Oh, and brushes of course!"

"Fabric to make new curtains!" said Hannah. "I could ask my mum if she could help us with that."

"This could all work out really well actually. . ." Charly said.

"How do you mean?" Meg asked.

"To get the hall really looking good, I mean!" Charly explained. "I mean, it's OK but it's not exactly a super-cool place to hang out, is it? With those boring green walls. . ."

"And those dreary curtains," Zoe agreed.

"So, this could be our chance to give it a real makeover!" Charly grinned.

"Nice one!" Zoe laughed.

"Cool!" Hannah said. "We could have a girls' zone at one end with beanbags to sit on!"

"Oh, Jack would love that!" Meg giggled.

"Well, he could go in the boys' zone!" Hannah suggested as a joke.

"Actually," Zoe said. "That's not such a silly idea!"

"No!" Flo laughed. "And it would be really great if we could have a mural on one of the walls. I've always wanted to do one of those."

"Fantastic idea!" Charly said.

"We've *got* to speak to Danny about this tomorrow!" Meg said, scribbling everything down fast.

"Go Glitter!" her friends agreed.

Chapter 5

On Friday night, the Glitter Girls were some of the first to arrive at the church hall.

"This place isn't much more exciting than the community hall," Flo said, looking round at the plain beige walls and drab grey curtains.

"Hey, we've only got time for one painting party!" Zoe grinned at her friend.

"Hang on a minute you two," Meg laughed, "we haven't even checked it out with Danny yet!"

The Glitter Girls gave each other excited looks and then grabbed seats to sit down and wait for Friday night's Energy Zone to begin properly.

"OK – so has anyone got any news to report?" Danny asked once everyone had arrived.

"We wanted to tell you about a brilliant idea we've had!" Zoe looked at her four friends as she spoke.

"Now why do I get the feeling that we're about to hear about some major project from you lot!" Danny grinned, knowing only too well the Glitter Girls' reputation for bright ideas. "Go on then."

"We thought we could have a painting party!" Flo said excitedly.

"Then we could all decorate the hall in the week before Easter!" added Hannah.

"Give it a proper makeover!" Charly put in eagerly.

"You know – like *Hit Squad*," said Meg.

"Then we could get the hall ready and still be able to have the Fun Day!" finished Zoe.

All around them, the other members of the Energy Zone were beginning to murmur enthusiastically at the Glitter Girls' idea.

"And you see, we could all help get it sorted

because the week before Easter is the school holidays!" Meg reported.

"Hmm," Danny scratched his chin thoughtfully. "It's a good idea – but it's a tall order." He looked round the room at the rest of the Energy Zone. "What does everyone else think?" he asked.

Immediately, the room was filled with a buzz of excitement as all the members of the Energy Zone started coming up with ideas for redecorating the hall.

"Hey, hey!" Danny said, waving his hands to quieten everyone down. "Sounds like this is something that you all want to do!"

"Yes!" everyone agreed.

"Right, well in that case –" Danny got his clipboard out and started to scribble things down on it – "it seems to me that we ought to check with the council to see if it would be OK for us to do the decorating. . ."

"Yes!"

"Danny?" Senami asked. "How about we ask the other people – you know, all the clubs and stuff that use the hall – ask them what they'd like done to make the hall better for them?"

"Good idea!" said Meg, wishing she'd thought of that too.

"It's certainly a good idea," Danny agreed. "But! Big but! First of all, we need to find out if the work really will be finished in time. If it is, then maybe they'll let us decorate. If it isn't. . ."

"Oh!" Everyone was downhearted just at the thought.

"But we could start to get organized just in case!" Meg suggested, pulling out her own notebook, ready to make notes on their action plan.

Danny laughed. "OK – you win," he said, as everyone cheered their approval. "We can start to make some plans but don't get too excited. I still need to check with the council and I won't be able to do that until Monday morning."

"Hey, Danny," said Charly. "We had this idea about a girls' zone and a boys' one."

"How does that work then?" Jack asked suspiciously.

Meg explained the Glitter Girls' idea.

"Sounds great!" Ria agreed.

"If it keeps you girls out of our way then it does!" Nick said.

Danny laughed. "It does sound like a cool idea."

"So if we're going to have a boys' zone and a girls' zone," Jack said, "can the boys be left alone to decorate our bit?"

"Well, there's no way the girls are going to help you!" Zoe joked.

"Fine by us," said Nick, "we don't want soppy girls putting pink stuff on our area."

"Yuck!" all the boys agreed.

"Settle down, you lot," Danny warned. "Actually, I think it would be a good idea if the boys did their own area and you girls did yours.

But what you need is a proper plan."

"What kind of plan?" Jack asked.

"A drawing of what the hall will look like when we're finished!" Flo said. "I'd love to do that!"

"Looks like the job's yours, then!" Danny smiled. "Right. I think that's as far as we can take our discussions tonight. So, what do you lot want to do for the rest of the evening?"

The Glitter Girls were just going to have to wait to find out if their painting party could really happen!

Chapter 6

RAT-tat-tat!

It was Saturday afternoon and Zoe didn't need to ask who was at her door as she listened to the familiar Glitter Girls' knock. She quickly opened the door and welcomed her four best friends in.

"Help yourself!" Zoe nodded towards a plateful of doughnuts on her desk and sat down to munch one herself.

"Mmm, great," said Flo. "Listen, I've been doing the plan with Kim this morning." She pulled a large drawing pad from her pink rucksack and showed the sketch to her friends.

"Hey – that looks great!" Charly said.

"This is the area I thought could be the boys'

zone," Flo pointed out. "And this is ours."

"And is this where the mural will be?" Charly asked. "If Danny agrees?"

"More like if the council agree," Meg pointed out.

"True. . ." Flo said.

"What about the colour of the other walls and the curtains and stuff?" Hannah asked.

"Yes – what do you all think?" Meg asked. She pulled out her notebook and pen from her purple bag.

"It would be best if the background colour to the main bits of the hall was fairly plain and simple," Flo suggested.

"How about pink?" said Zoe, looking around at the gorgeous pink walls of her own room.

"Cool," agreed Hannah.

"Only the boys probably won't like that, will they?" Charly pointed out.

"We'd better ask Danny if the council will let us choose," suggested Meg. "After all, we don't even know if we're allowed to have the painting party yet."

"But we can still hope for it, can't we?" Hannah urged. "I mean – I really hope we can replace those horrible old curtains!"

All her friends laughed. "I agree," said Flo. "But I've been thinking – where are we going to get all the money to pay for new curtains and paint?"

"And who's going to make the curtains?" Charly added.

"Well, there must be some money from the council put aside to repaint the hall, mustn't there?" Meg said.

"And my mum has already said that she will help us out with the curtains!" Hannah grinned.

"Nice one!" Zoe said. "Do you think she could help us out with other things for the girls' zone as well?"

"Yes," beamed Flo. "That would be really

great – she's just so good at that sort of stuff."

"I'm sure she could be persuaded!" Hannah laughed.

"So what about the mural, Flo?" Meg asked.

With a flourish, Flo turned to the next page of her sketchpad and presented a fantastic design to her friends. It was a sea of people from the Energy Zone.

"This is great!" exclaimed Zoe. "But how on earth are we going to be able to paint it all?"

"I thought I'd ask Kim if she could help me get the basic design outlined on the wall," Flo explained. "Then each of us could select a person and that way we can get the outline filled in."

"What if we all want to do the same person?" Hannah asked.

"I know!" Meg said, starting to write what she was saying down in her notebook. "We could put all the names in a hat and whoever's name you pull out you have to paint!"

"Hey, that's a really good idea, Meg. This is going to be just great, Flo!" said Charly. "You are brilliant!"

The other Glitter Girls agreed and Meg gave Flo a hug.

"Oh," said Hannah. "I don't think I can bear to wait until Monday to find out what the council says."

"Nor me," agreed Zoe.

"Yes," said Meg, "and if the council does say yes, there's going to be a *lot* to do before Fun Day, isn't there?"

Chapter 7

Absolutely everyone turned up at the Energy Zone on Monday night, eager to find out what Danny had to report.

"Can everyone grab a seat?" Danny asked first. Once everyone had settled down he began. "OK, I rang the council—"

"What did they say?" almost everyone cried at once.

"Quieten down, you lot!" Danny laughed. "The council said we can do it—"

There were loud cheers from everyone in the hall.

"*But!*" Danny waved his hands at everyone for quiet. "There are a couple of things that they're insisting on!"

"What?" Meg wanted to know.

"Well, for a start we've only got five days to complete the project," Danny explained. "We come in on the Monday and *have* to be finished by the Friday afternoon."

"We can do that easily, can't we?" Nick said confidently.

The others mumbled their agreement.

"Well, it will be a lot of hard work," Danny warned. "But if you lot get cracking on it and don't muck about then, yes, I think we might be able to get it sorted."

"Yesss!" came the response from around the hall.

"I've asked my friend Joe if he can come and help us out," Danny added. "He's the teacher I was telling you about."

"So what else is the council asking us to do?" Ria wondered.

"We've got to make sure that we include all the other people who use the hall," Danny explained. "You know – the art club, the toddler group, people like that."

"But it was the Energy Zone's project!" Charly spluttered. "We want to paint it!"

Other people around the hall agreed with her.

Danny laughed. "I know you lot are mad keen to do it! But don't worry – the council doesn't necessarily want them all to help you out."

"Well, what do they want, then?" Flo demanded.

"They just want us to speak with them all – find out what sort of things they'd like to find in the newly decorated hall before we go off and change things."

"Phew!" Zoe sighed in relief.

"So who are all these people?" Senami asked.

"My little sister comes to the playgroup here," Charly explained. "It's called Teddies. Should I ask my mum to check with all the other parents?"

"Thing is, if we've got to go around town and

speak to everyone who uses the hall, it'll take us absolutely ages," said Fizz.

"Yes!" muttered everyone in agreement.

"I know!" said Meg, efficient as ever. "Why don't we draw up a quick questionnaire? Then we could give it to them all and ask for their answers by the end of the week!"

"Brilliant idea, Meg," Danny agreed. "And it just so happens that I had the very same idea myself! I drew up a questionnaire and printed some out at school – I brought a whole load of them with me tonight."

"Right," said Zoe. "So we just need to give them out to all the groups."

"Yes, and I've got a list of them as well as contact names for each one that the council provided," Danny said. He held up the list.

"Who are the Salsatinas?" asked Hannah, peering at the list.

"The Salsa class," said Nicole, one of the older girls. "My mum goes – I'll give some to her."

"Thanks," said Danny. "Now, we need a couple of people to send the rest out to the astronomy society, the Green Fingers gardening association, the toddler group . . . and the 'Artful Splodgers' – I'm guessing that's the art class!"

"I'll do it," volunteered Chenzira. "And Senami can give me a hand, OK?"

Senami nodded at her friend.

"And someone will need to collect all the replies," suggested Meg.

"We can do that too," Senami said eagerly.

"Well, that's sorted then," Danny said. "Now we've just got the rest of the painting party to organize!"

"We're going to need paint!" Flo said. "Lots of bright paint!"

"But how are we going to pay for it?" Ria asked.

"The council's giving us a small budget for paint," Danny explained. "It's probably easiest to go to the DIY shop in town."

"Can we use any colours we want?" Flo asked eagerly.

"Yes, I think so, but bear in mind that there's not a huge amount of money," Danny warned. "We need to be careful we don't spend it all on paint!"

"I know!" said Zoe. "Why don't we ask the local paper if they'll put something in about the painting party? They already did an article about the hall being flooded."

"Well the newspaper's not going to sort the paint for us, is it?" Jack said, and he and Nick laughed. *"Duh!"*

"Actually," Meg said. "It's not such a silly idea to get the newspaper to print something! They could tell everyone what we are doing and ask for donations from people."

"Yes!" agreed Zoe. "Like asking for new crockery and other stuff to jazz the place up a bit!"

"Maybe we could persuade local shops to help us out?" Hannah suggested.

"Yes!" came the agreement around the hall.

"OK," said Danny, "I like it! It's certainly worth a try. Would you girls be prepared to go to the newspaper and have a word with them?"

"Go Glitter!" came their enthusiastic reply.

★ ♥ ★ ♥ ★ ♥ ★

The Glitter Girls went straight round to the newspaper office after school on Tuesday afternoon.

"Don't be too long," Mrs Fisher warned, leaving them in the office reception while she went off to do some shopping with Lily, Charly's younger sister.

"Well, if it isn't the Glitter Girls!" the receptionist smiled at them. "What can we do for you today?"

Meg explained to her about the painting party.

"Sounds like you need to speak to one of the reporters!" the girl said. "Wait here and I'll just find someone for you to talk to."

A few minutes later, the receptionist returned with a friendly young woman whom the Glitter Girls recognized.

"Hello, girls," she said warmly. "I'm Sara. Do you remember me? I remember you lot – from the school fête in the summer. You did a lovely job on my nails at the Magical Makeovers stall!"

"Oh yes!" the Glitter Girls cried, glad to be talking to a friendly face. They quickly began to explain the help they needed to get the painting party off the ground.

"I'm sure everyone will be delighted to help!" Sara agreed, once she'd heard the whole story. "I'll put a list of the things you've mentioned in the article and. . ." she winked at them, "I'll see if we can mention this story on the front page!"

"That would be great!" cried Meg.

"Well – look out for it on Thursday!" Sara grinned.

"Go Glitter!"

Chapter 8

On Thursday afternoon, Dr Baker, Zoe's mum, met the Glitter Girls from school.

"Thought you'd like to see this!" she said, handing them a copy of the local newspaper.

"Hey, excellent!" Meg exclaimed as she caught sight of one of the stories on the front page.

"What does it say?" Flo wanted to know.

" 'It's High Energy as the Glitter Girls Zone in on the Community Hall!' " Charly read aloud.

"Now that's what I call a story," Hannah said as she and the other girls read through what Sara had written.

"This is just what we needed to get everyone's support for the painting party!" Zoe declared.

"And Fun Day!" Charly added. "Danny's going to be really pleased!"

"What else have we got to organize for next week?" Flo asked. "After all, we break up tomorrow and then the work really starts!"

"We need a meeting," Meg said, flicking her long curly hair away from her face.

"Tell you what, girls," Dr Baker suggested as she pulled in to the estate where all the Glitter Girls lived. "How about you have the meeting while I make you all some tea?"

"Go Glitter!" the girls all said in reply.

★ ♥ ★ ♥ ★ ♥ ★

Ten minutes later the Glitter Girls were settled and comfy in Zoe's bedroom, ready to talk about their action plan.

"I've had an idea about the girls' zone," Flo began.

"What?" Hannah asked.

"I thought we could sort of paint it pink and

maybe paint some stars and stuff on it with a stencil," she explained.

"That sounds cool," Charly said.

"Sounds cool to me too but we'll have to persuade Danny, won't we?" said Meg, writing it down on her list.

"Hey – Mum said I could go through all her fabric oddments and choose any bits we need to make cushion covers and stuff," Hannah declared.

"Excellent," said Flo. She grinned at her friend, thinking just how gorgeous the girls' zone was going to be.

"I'm not sure I'm good enough at art to do my bit on the mural," Charly confessed, pushing up her glasses. "I'm not nearly as good at painting as you are, Flo."

"Nor me," Meg agreed.

"No worries," Flo reassured them. "Kim's definitely going to help me out. She's going to come along and help me sketch out the mural on the wall from a scale drawing we've made. All you'll have to worry about is one figure and it doesn't matter if it's not perfect – that's the point."

"That sounds so good," Hannah said, hugging her friend.

"Girls?"

It was Dr Baker calling them from downstairs.

"Meeting over?" Meg suggested, closing her notebook and putting it back in her rucksack. "I'm starving and I think we're all organized anyway!"

"Go Glitter!" her friends replied.

The Energy Zone was packed on Friday night. They were all making a special trip to the community hall to see how it was coming along.

"What a mess!" Nick exclaimed when they got inside.

He was right! The floor was covered in a layer of dust and old newspapers. The windows were grimy with dirt and the whole place looked sad and grey.

"This is a tip!" sighed Hannah.

"Can we ever get this straight?" Charly asked. The place was in such a state she wondered if even with the whole of the Energy Zone involved they'd be able to get the hall ready in just five days.

"It's a dump!" Jack declared. "I thought it was meant to have been sorted out!"

"Well, it was hardly going to look like some perfect room out of a catalogue or something, was it? That's the point – we're going to make it better," Meg said, thinking how dumb her brother could be sometimes.

"But it's going to take us ages to get this place looking cool," Nick said, agreeing with Jack.

"But like Meg says – that's why we're here, isn't it?" Flo pointed out.

"Exactly!" said Danny. "Come on, cheer up you lot! Listen – the newspaper article has brought us lots of results!"

"Yes!" everyone cried, feeling happier.

"We've got lots of odd tins of paint from the DIY store. . ."

"That means we can paint each wall a different colour!" grinned Flo.

". . .and the Crock Shop has promised us some new mugs and plates and stuff. . ."

"Cool!" said Amy.

". . .then there's some pieces of carpet coming from Underfoot and some new lamp shades, beanbags and cushions from Furnish U."

"Great!" everyone cheered.

"Oh – and lastly, the chemist's in town has sent me a couple of party cameras so that we can make an album of memories! I thought Flo could take some!"

"Oh!" Nick moaned. "I could do that!"

"You can have the other one, Nick," said Danny, grinning. "So, Chenzira and Senami, how did you get on with the questionnaires?"

The two girls reported that Teddies asked for cupboard space for their toys and stuff but other than that, everyone had simply said that the place needed cheering up and they'd be happy with that.

"Good!" Danny smiled. "Well, it looks like it's all on track! But before we go around town putting up posters about Fun Day, I just need to remind you all about Monday."

Everyone was keen to listen.

"I want you all here at nine prompt! You'll need old clothes and shoes that you won't mind getting dirty," Danny said to a murmur of approval from the boys especially.

"What about the paint?" Meg asked.

"That's going to be delivered on Monday," Danny confirmed. "So just make sure you are all there on time!"

Everyone was so keen to help out that no one was late on the Monday morning. It was a dreary, cloudy morning and the hall looked just as miserable as it had on Friday night.

The Glitter Girls had swapped their usual denim jackets for old jeans and T-shirts. To protect their hair from the paint Charly and Flo had piled theirs up on top of their heads, Meg was wearing an old baseball cap and Zoe and Hannah were wearing headscarves.

"Now this I have to take a photo of!" Flo said, pulling the camera out of her bag. "I've got to take a picture of everyone before the transformation!"

"Great idea!" Danny said. "Come on, everyone – line up and say 'cheese'!"

Everyone collapsed with laughter as they all gathered at one end of the hall.

"OK – bags and kit under this dust sheet to

keep them clean," Danny declared, covering everything up. "The paint's already arrived, so let's see what colours we've got!"

A glance through the tins and the Energy Zone was decided. One wall was going to be orange, another bright blue and the third one green!"

"Just don't forget to leave the mural white!" Flo warned. "Oh – and we can choose the paints for the boys' and girls' zones later!"

"Let's paint, then!" Danny yelled, switching on the CD player he'd brought with him and turning up the volume. "Tea and choccy biscuits when we've finished this wall!"

The girls began singing along with the music as they painted – the painting party had begun!

★ ♥ ★ ♥ ★ ♥ ★

"Danny? When can we have a break?" Jack whined about ten minutes later. "This is hard work!"

"Lightweight!" Flo giggled.

"I don't think so!" Jack said, flicking some paint in the Glitter Girls' direction.

"Hey, watch it you lot!" Danny yelled as the paint splattered his face instead of the Glitter Girls.

"Well, she said I was a lightweight!" Jack said defensively, flicking some more paint that landed on Meg's baseball cap.

"Everyone knows that girls are better at stuff than boys!" Charly declared.

All the girls in the room murmured their approval.

"Not true!" Nick called.

"Out of order!" came the calls of disagreement from the rest of the boys.

"OK then, you lot," Danny said, standing back for a minute. "Let's find out, shall we?"

"How?" Meg asked.

"Let's have all the boys on this side of me," said Danny, pointing to his left. "And all the girls on the other."

"OK?" he asked when they were lined up. "Right – I'll count from ten and then you all start painting your side up to here." Danny painted a line just in front of him. "Then we can see whether it is the boys or the girls who finish first!"

"Boys!"

"Girls!" came the declarations.

"Ten! Nine! Eight! Seven! Six! Five! Four! Three! Two! One!"

The race was on!

Chapter 9

An hour later, there were screams above the music.

"Winner!" yelled Nick.

"Finished!" screamed the Glitter Girls.

Danny laughed and climbed down from the ladder where he had been busily painting above everyone's heads.

"Looks to me like a draw!" Danny giggled.

"Cop out!" Jack declared.

"That's no way fair!" agreed Zoe, who was convinced that the girls' side had really won.

"Well I think the winner is really the wall," Danny said. "I think it looks pretty good."

Everyone stepped back and admired their hard work.

"Come on," Danny suggested, "let's take a tea break and we'll have a rematch with the next wall after that!"

The morning passed quickly and by the time everyone sat down to enjoy their picnic lunch, two large walls in the hall were looking fresh and finished.

"So do you think we'll be finished in time for Fun Day?" Meg asked Danny as Flo took another photo of them all and Nick larked about taking pictures of the boys being stupid.

"Well – as long as we don't have any disasters, it should be OK," Danny confirmed, as a piece of bread flew past his ear. "Who threw that? Let me guess – Jack?"

Judging from the giggling going on, Jack was indeed the culprit.

"If you've got that much energy, Jack," Danny grinned. "Then let's get going on the last two walls."

"And this time the girls will win!" Senami declared, leading the rush to get painting again.

★ ♥ ★ ♥ ★ ♥ ★

By the end of Monday; the four main walls had been painted and Danny declared the second wall another draw, the girls the winners of the third wall and the boys the winners of the fourth, so overall it was a kind of draw. But the hall was no way near finished.

"Even with the paint on the walls it still looks like a dump!" Zoe sighed, as the Glitter Girls walked home with Mrs Fisher.

"I know," Hannah agreed, twiddling her hair in her fingers.

"There's just so much to do," Charlie said, pushing her glasses back up.

"Do you think we can do it?" Flo wondered.

"Of course we can!" Meg said, determined as ever. "We're the Glitter Girls, aren't we?"

"Go Glitter!" her friends confirmed.

★ ♥ ★ ♥ ★ ♥ ★

The sun was shining on Tuesday morning and it broke through the windows covering the hall in a warm light.

"Now this looks better!" said Meg, running into the hall with her friends.

"Hi girls!" Danny smiled. "This is Joe, by the way – he's finally turned up to help us!"

"Hi gang!" Joe smiled. "You're doing a great job!"

"So, Flo," said Danny. "Are you going to start the mural today?"

"Certainly am!" Flo confirmed. "Kim's going to be here soon to help me."

"So what are we going to do?" Charly wanted to know.

"Well, you can either help the boys paint a second coat on that wall over there –" Danny pointed to the opposite wall where a group of boys were already painting away – "or you might want to clean up the windows on the porch doors and trying painting with this." Danny led them over to the tins of paint and showed them some special paint that had been donated. The paint was translucent so that the light shone through and created a really pretty stained-glass-window effect.

"Cool – I've used this before with stencils!" Hannah said.

"Let's do it, then!" Meg said.

The morning's work had begun!

An hour or so later, the Glitter Girls were chatting away with the other girls from the Energy Zone. They had been busy helping to clean up the kitchen area that was hidden behind a door at one end of the hall. Meg was explaining to them about the fabrics and ideas that they had for the girls' zone.

"We thought we could maybe make a kind of patchwork throw thing which we could either hang up or maybe sit on," Hannah said.

"Cool!" Amy said, and it was clear that the other girls agreed with her.

"What colour are we going to paint the walls?" Senami asked.

"I've been looking through the tins of paint and I found this scrummy stuff," Flo held up a tin and grinned. "It's glitter paint! There's some pink- and some lavender-coloured paint too!"

"We could make a girls' heaven!" Chenzira exclaimed.

"Hey, look at this!" said Charly. "It says on the tin that it glows like stars in the night!"

"We should get Danny to paint the ceiling with that, then!" Flo said.

"Have we got everything we need?" Meg wanted to know.

"It's great – just perfect," Flo declared.

But their fun was interrupted by Joe.

"Come on, there's work to do!" he laughed.

Wednesday brought more sunshine and the Glitter Girls arrived feeling that they had indeed made some progress the day before. Hannah's mum had come with them – she'd brought her sewing machine with her to make up the curtains.

"Phew!" she said. "I hope you lot are going to help me! There's a lot of windows in this place!"

"Do you think there'll be time?" Hannah asked, feeling worried about how much there was to do.

Mrs Giles ruffled her daughter's long red hair. "I should think we'll manage with all this team-work going on!"

"Morning all!" Danny declared from the top of his ladder. The Glitter Girls, with the help of the rest of the Energy Zone, had managed to persuade Danny to paint the ceiling with the special paint.

"I reckon it will look best if we just use it to paint a moon and some stars with – it'll be more effective that way!" Joe said, from his ladder on the other side of the room.

"Wow, that's going to be fantastic!" Mrs Giles said, as she put her sewing machine down.

"Thank the Glitter Girls! It was one of their great ideas!" Danny said, winking at them.

Flo beamed. "It was just that we had this great paint given to us," she said. "You know – it glows in the dark and it was just perfect for making fluorescent clouds and starry stuff!"

"No time to waste, everyone!" Danny warned. "Girls – you get to do your zone today! Boys! You're over in your corner! The team that does the best job wins a prize!"

"Go Glitter!" the five friends screamed, and rushed to begin!

Chapter 10

"OK," Flo whispered to all the girls who were gathered in their zone. "I haven't got time to help you much – Kim and I have still got loads to do for the mural. But I thought you could paint the background pink with maybe the lavender as the border? Then you could give a topcoat of this glitter finish which would look cool."

"Nice one!" Hannah agreed.

"So do we do straight lines down the side here?" Amy indicated towards the edges of the zone.

"No – I think it'd look really nice if there were sort of wavy lines down either side of our zone like this," Flo showed the girls what she meant on her sketch pad.

"OK, let's get going," Zoe hissed. "The boys have already started!"

Over in their zone, the boys had begun to paint a sludgy green colour on the walls.

"I heard Jack talking with Nick on the phone last night," Meg whispered. "They're going to make it look like an army camp!"

"Boys will be boys!" Charly tutted, fiddling with her glasses.

And all the girls, the Glitter Girls included, giggled in agreement.

Over by the entrance wall, Kim and Flo were starting to colour in the outline sketches. It was taking them a long time but if you stood at the other side of the hall, you could see just how fantastic the finished mural was going to be. Every now and then, Flo popped over to the girls' zone to see how they were getting on.

"Don't paint the glitter on too soon!" she warned. "Otherwise the colours will run!"

"It's looking OK, isn't it?" Meg asked.

"Fab!" said Ria, and the other girls agreed with her.

By lunchtime, everyone was exhausted. The boys were being more irritating than ever, telling the girls that not only were they nearly finished but also that their zone was definitely going to be the best.

"Fat chance!" Hannah poked her tongue out at them.

"You'll see!" Jack warned.

"Now then, boys and girls!" Danny wagged his finger at them all jokingly. "I'll be the judge of that!"

"How are the curtains coming on, Mrs Giles?" asked Zoe.

"Well, I've done the cutting out and started on the sewing but I'm going to need some help later on if that's possible," she replied.

"Who's going to be able to help?" Danny asked, looking round.

"We can!" Meg said, volunteering all of the girls. "We need to wait for our paint to dry before we can do anything else."

"What about you lot?" Danny asked the boys.

"We're not doing any sewing!" Jack said defiantly. "That's for girls!"

"Actually, I've got another job for you anyway!" Joe declared. "We need you to sweep up the muck outside by the entrance, OK?"

"Oh, *great!*" the boys replied.

The Glitter Girls laughed amongst themselves – they knew Jack would prefer sewing to that boring chore!

"Come on," Danny urged. "No time for wasters round here! There's more work to do."

"Come on!" Meg whispered to all of the girls. "Let's take a look at their zone while they're outside!"

With the boys safely out of the way, they sneaked over.

"Hey – it's actually quite cool!" Chenzira declared.

The boys had made the whole thing look like a real den. They'd put cupboards on either side of their area to make it enclosed and someone had brought an old camouflage net in, to hang between the cupboards making a kind of entrance.

"They're certainly going to keep things secret in there," Hannah said.

"Do you think it's better than our zone?" Amy asked.

The girls all went back to their zone. It did look a bit bare and exposed.

"The colours are great," said Senami.

"But we need to make it more secret!" Charly sighed.

"Problem, girls?" said Mrs Giles. She had come over with the curtain material ready to hem.

The Glitter Girls explained.

"I see what you mean," Mrs Giles said thoughtfully. "Tell you what – why don't we hang up some gauze? It would just keep things covered up enough to make them more secret. I could easily attach it to the ceiling with some curtain wire I've got in my workbasket."

"That would be great, but where are we going to get gauze from?" Flo wondered.

"I've got some at home," Mrs Giles said. "Why don't I bring it in tomorrow? The thing is, you Glitter Girls will have to help me hem it tonight!"

"Go Glitter!" the five best friends agreed.

"Great!" said Chenzira.

"Smile!" said Flo. And another photo was taken for the album!

Thursday was spent putting the finishing touches to the mural. Meg had written every-one's name on a piece of paper and the first thing everyone had to do on Thursday morning was pull a name out of one of Joe's old baseball caps.

"I've got Jack to paint!" Charly giggled.

"And I've got Danny!" said Meg.

"I'm doing Chenzira," Hannah said.

"Hey, I've got to paint you, Meg!" giggled Flo.

"Fizz," sighed Zoe.

Everyone enjoyed painting in the outlines Flo and Kim had done.

"It's looking really good!" Flo said, smiling as she went round the hall taking more photos. Nick was also taking photos but they seemed to be mainly of Jack pulling dumb faces!

"So's the girls' zone," said Meg, who, along with the other girls, had been helping Mrs Giles put up their gauze screen. The Glitter Girls had spent a very giggly evening at Hannah's house the night before, hemming the curtain under Mrs Giles's instruction.

"There's something missing," Meg declared, when the girls thought they had finished.

They'd put up great posters on the walls and spread lots of cushions around but it still didn't look quite good enough.

"Yes – I know what you mean," Hannah said.

"We need more stuff – you know, to make it look more comfy," suggested Emily.

"You're right," Charly confirmed. "We need to make it look more like our bedrooms – these chairs look so sort of formal."

"Yes it looks more like a waiting room than somewhere cool," Flo said.

"I know!" Hannah declared. "We could add more floor-cushions and decorate them with sequins and stuff – make them look more glitzy!"

"I could bring some magazines in from home," Ria suggested.

"That's exactly the sort of stuff we need," Meg said. "Books would be good too, and maybe some games!"

Just then the boys came over.

"You lot finished then?" Jack said sarcastically. "It doesn't look that great to me."

"Our zone's not finished yet!" Meg said defiantly. "What about you?"

"Oh, we're cool!" said Nick.

The boys had put a sign on the entrance to their tent thing. It read GIRLS KEEP OUT!

"Huh!" Zoe muttered secretly to the other girls when the boys had gone to eat their lunch. "We've just got to make it look better than this!"

★ ❤ ★ ❤ ★ ❤ ★

The delivery men from the carpet shop arrived on Thursday afternoon, bringing a marvellous selection of goodies.

"This lot's great!" Danny said, thanking them on behalf of the Energy Zone.

There was all sorts of stuff – rugs, little mats that were perfect for Teddies – even some stuff that looked like grass!

"Got it!" said Ria, pulling out a fabulous soft purple rug. "This is just what we need for our zone!"

"Brilliant!" said Flo. "Let's put it in there now!"

The rest of the afternoon was spent finishing off the curtains with Mrs Giles. Because they'd said sewing was for girls, Mrs Giles got the boys to do the hemming while the girls were given the job of screwing in the curtain hooks and then helping Danny to hang them. Jack and Nick didn't stop moaning!

"There," Danny said at the end of the day. "It's really beginning to look great!"

"So who's going to win the prize?" Jack wanted to know.

"Hmm," Danny mused. "It's going to be a difficult decision . . . but I'll let you know when we're done."

"Huh!" hissed Charly to the other Glitter Girls. "It's obvious that the girls' zone is going to win!"

Chapter 11

Friday morning was a frantic blur of activity. There was no time for any mucking about as Danny and Joe moved all the main cupboards and storage boxes back into their positions and then the Energy Zone neatly filled them with their contents.

The girls spent a frantic morning sewing decorations on to their cushions while the boys were organized to clean the floor as well as put all the sparkling new, brightly coloured crockery into the kitchen area.

"Our zone looks great now!" Meg declared approvingly as the last of the cushions was put into place. "Everything does!" She looked around the hall and admired their handiwork.

Everything in the hall looked and smelt new and clean.

At last, everyone was grateful to sit down for the picnic lunch.

"So," Danny said when they were finished. "We've got to get things ready for Fun Day! I'll do the treasure hunt tomorrow with Joe. But I could do with some help getting the area at the back ready for the barbecue."

"Oh no!" the Glitter Girls all cried collectively.

"What's the nightmare?" Danny asked jokingly.

"Decorating the hall!" Meg said. "We'd forgotten all about it!"

With all the things to remember for the painting party, the Glitter Girls had completely forgotten that they had promised to decorate the hall ready for the disco on Saturday night!

"Ha, ha!" Jack said. "Not so perfect after all, are you?"

"It's not a problem!" Zoe said, not sounding

at all convinced. "We've got plenty of time to do it this afternoon!"

"Have we?" Charly hissed to Zoe after Jack had gone off to find Nick.

"Course we have!" Flo said, popping her thumb into her mouth as she always did when she was tired or thinking.

"But we haven't done our eggs either!" whispered Hannah.

"We'll just have to rush round and do everything after lunch!" Meg said.

The Glitter Girls hardly had time to stop. Mrs Giles raced them all home so that they could gather together their families' Christmas fairy lights.

"This isn't going to be enough stuff to make a hall that size look good!" Flo sighed as they were standing in Zoe's garage collecting the last of the lights.

"I know!" Meg said confidently. "We need to

make paper chains – I've got some coloured paper at home!"

"And we could put up balloons – I'm sure we've got some left over from Lily's birthday party!" Charly declared.

"Go Glitter!" her friends agreed, and they set off to gather everything else they needed.

★ ♥ ★ ♥ ★ ♥ ★

By seven o'clock that night, the hall was completely transformed. Gone was the grubby, depressing building that the Energy Zone had started with on Monday morning to be replaced by the sparkling, glittery place that it was now! When the overhead lights were switched off and the fairy lights switched on, the Glitter Girls gazed in wonder as the hall shimmered in the evening light.

"Doesn't the ceiling look great?" Meg said, looking up at the night sky that Danny and Joe had created at Flo's suggestion.

"Perfect!" Hannah agreed. "Just perfect!"

★ ♥ ★ ♥ ★ ♥ ★

Even the Glitter Girls were too tired to work on their eggs that night. So on Saturday morning, they met really early in Hannah's mum's workroom. Just like they'd planned, they found the eggs they'd begun all those weeks ago and then, using scraps of wool to match their own hair colouring, lots of gel pens, and bits of denim to make jackets, they each made an egg that looked like themselves!

"There's no time to embroider the back of the jackets," Meg sighed.

"We can write GG on with pink fabric paint!" Hannah suggested.

"Do you think we'll win?" Charly asked as she wrote.

"Don't know," Zoe said, putting a name label into the big box that Hannah's mum had given them to put their eggs in. "Maybe if we'd had more time to think about it we might have. But the painting party was more important."

Meg looked at her watch. It was nearly lunchtime. "Come on, it's time to get changed – we'll have to go soon!"

★　♥　★　♥　★　♥　★

The Glitter Girls had all changed into their favourite clothes. Hannah wore a pair of embroidered jeans and a really pretty top covered in flowers and edged with lace. Zoe had decided on her white gypsy-style skirt and a pink fitted jumper. Charly was wearing a pair of candy-striped trousers and a lilac-coloured shirt that matched perfectly. Meg had chosen her favourite denim skirt and a floaty blue top that was the same colour as her eyes, and Flo was wearing black cords and a soft, fluffy, pale blue jumper. They all looked fab!

By the time they arrived, the hall was already filling up with a steady stream of helpers.

Danny had put posters up outside the hall so no one could miss where the Fun Day was.

Inside, the sun was shining through the windows and the egg table was already beginning to fill up with decorated eggs. Placing their box carefully at one end, the Glitter Girls wandered round, saying hello to people and seeing where Will had set up the pool tournament. Jack and Nick had even got their kit ready for the disco that night. Outside, the barbecue was already set up in one corner of the Rec. Danny and Joe had put masses of flags and balloons all over the rest of the field.

"That must be for the treasure hunt!" Charly grinned.

"Hi, girls!" Danny said when he saw them. "There's a reporter here from the paper – she wants to have a word with you." He pointed towards the flags.

"OK," said the Glitter Girls, smiling at each other.

They saw Sara on the other side of the Rec and went over to say hi.

"Ahh! The Glitter Girls!" she declared. "You've done it again – everything looks brilliant!"

The Glitter Girls beamed.

"So, tell me all about the painting party," Sara said.

Between them, the five best friends explained all about their week-long painting party and how everyone at the Energy Zone had helped out by working so hard.

"And I've taken photos of the whole thing!" Flo explained. "I'm going to make an album of them together with Nick – another member of the Energy Zone – after they've been developed."

"Sounds like you've been busy then," Sara smiled. "Perhaps we could use some of your photos in the paper? I could get them developed for you if you like."

"Thanks!" Flo beamed.

"Now, I need to get everyone from the Energy Zone together. I want to take a photo for the paper myself!" Sara smiled.

"We'll get them!" Meg volunteered, and the Glitter Girls moved off in different directions to find their other friends.

★ ♥ ★ ♥ ★ ♥ ★

"OK, boys and girls?" Danny was standing in the middle of the Rec and using a megaphone to get everyone's attention. "Fun Day is now officially open! But before we all get carried away with too much fun, I just wanted to thank you all for the great work you've done this week. It's been a top job! And I think you all deserve a round of applause!"

The Energy Zone were delighted to clap for each other. The Glitter Girls hugged each other as well, thrilled that the painting party had been such a success.

"Oh, and just one more thing!" Danny said.

"The competition between the girls and the boys for the best zone!"

There was a hush as each group was eager to know who had won!

"It was hard! But. . ." Danny paused dramatically. Then he laughed and said, "Both zones are really great! So . . . it's another draw!"

"Fix!" Jack moaned.

"What's our prize?" Meg yelled to Danny across the field.

"You all get a free Easter egg from Choc City!" Danny replied. "Come on – let's get on with Fun Day!"

"Cool, thanks Danny!" Hannah said, and there was general agreement from the rest of the girls and boys.

"It's been great, hasn't it?" Meg said to her four best friends. The Rec was already crowded with people who had come to join in with Fun Day.

"Brilliant!" Charly said for them all.

"It still is!" said Hannah. "We've only just started and there's still the disco to come! I can't wait to have a dance!"

"I can't believe we actually did it! For a while there I never thought the Fun Day would happen," said Zoe happily.

"And we've got a gorgeous new hall too!" Flo looked around at her friends and smiled.

"Come on, we've got to beat Jack and Nick to the treasure!" Meg cried.

"Go Glitter!" the five best friends yelled and they ran off towards the beginning of the treasure hunt.